CW00847216

Melany-Jane and Oliver

For my
family and friends

Written and illustrated by Lynne Colclough

OLIVER was a large tortoise with a large problem.
He couldn't stay awake!

He slept in the road, on the path and even on the stairs!
His friend, Melany-Jane, was also tired.
She was tired of falling over him.

"Oh dear!" she said sharply "What are we going to do with you?"

But it was no use telling him off because he'd fallen asleep again.

"Well!" said Melany-Jane "How rude!" and she picked him up and
put him into the garden while she had her dinner.

ZZZzzz

Oliver woke up feeling cold. There was a draught whistling through his shell. *'Brrrr! No wonder'* he thought *'I'm outside.'*

There was a knock on his shell. He peeped out, which was difficult because the draught had given him a stiff neck.

A hedgehog was outside looking most agitated. "Would you mind moving off my leaves please?" it asked politely.

"Certainly" said Oliver, and did so "Why are you collecting leaves?" he asked.

"For a nest" said the hedgehop rapidly "Sorry, must dash. See you next spring."

"But why? Why? Ummm..." But whatever it was he was going to ask didn't get asked. Oliver was asleep again!

A few minutes later he woke with a shock.

'I'M FLYING!' he thought,

'well, jumping at least and it's none of my doing.'

He counted his legs. 'One, *two, umph! Ouph!*' It was always a bother turning in his shell to count his back legs, '*three, four,*' he managed at last. "No" he said "it's not me, all four legs are safe inside. Well I suppose I'd better find out what's going on."

He looked out.

There was a frog trying to dig under him!

"Hey you!" said Oliver "Stop that, go around me or over me even! But don't go under me."

The frog jumped backwards, forwards and sideways in surprise in fact he jumped so much that Oliver's stiff neck really hurt.

"Sorry!" said the frog "but I'm looking for a comfortable stone to hibernate under."

"I'm not a stone!" said Oliver horrified "I'm Oliver..."

"Well you did look like a rather superior stone" he said placatingly, he was going to carry on apologising but Oliver butted in

"And anyway what is a hibernate?"

"What is a hibernate?" repeated the frog "What is a hibernate? It isn't an anything. It's something some animals do in the winter. We find somewhere cosy and sleep until spring." he looked at Oliver who was yawning.

"That's what you should be doing."

"What!' said Oliver incredulously "Crawling under stones?"

"No!" said the frog "Hibernating!"

"What!
   Crawling under stones?"

"How can you tell when to hibernate?" asked Oliver.

"How can you tell? How can you tell?" repeated the frog

"Look around you! Look around you!"

Oliver tried to look around but his stiff neck
prevented him.

"Err, what am I looking for?"
he asked innocently.

"My, my, you really know nothing" said the
exasperated frog "Look at the leaves, when
the leaves change colour it's a sign winter is
coming. Look at the weather can't you feel it
getting colder. Look at the time! I must be
flying. See you next spring."

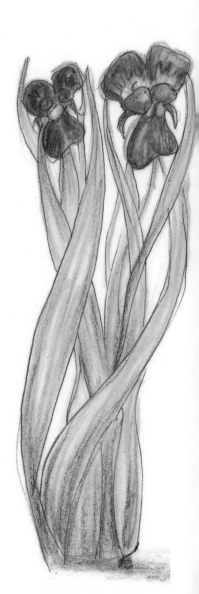

Melany-Jane found Oliver awake and
concentrating hard "What's the matter Oliver?"
she asked, and then she laughed (well you
would too if you saw a tortoise concentrating).

"I'm trying to think of a place to hibernate"
he said crossly.

"Oh!" said Melany-Jane and sat down next to
him and concentrated too.

"How can you tell when
to hibernate?"

She could think where hedgehogs hibernated, where squirrels hibernated, but couldn't for the life of her think where a tortoise was supposed to go. "Perhaps" she said at last "you aren't supposed to hibernate" but Oliver was asleep so he didn't hear her "Oh wake up Oliver!" she said crossly. She thought again. "I've got an idea!" she decided "Since we can't think of a special place for you, how about trying out the other animals places and see if any of them suit you."

"Well" said Oliver, he wasn't too keen on the idea "I don't fancy being stuck under a stone all winter so I don't think I'll try that."

Melany-Jane agreed it didn't sound very comfortable.

"I suppose we could try the old rabbit burrow at the bottom
of the garden."

"I beg your pardon?" questioned Oliver

"What could we try the
old burrow for?"

*"For sticking you
down, silly!"* she said.

Oliver was shocked "I don't think I like that idea either."

"You don't know until you've tried it" she said.

Oliver sulked "Don't mind me I've only got to live down there."

"Hedgehogs and mice and things all find it quite cosy so why shouldn't you?" and before he could argue anymore she tucked him under her arm and went and put her wellies on.

When they found the hole Melany-Jane had to admit it didn't look all that cosy. 'Still, it might look better from the inside' she thought.

She put Oliver down "go inside and find a comfortable place and I'll collect some leaves to keep you warm" she said. Oliver did not reply, he was still sulking, nevertheless he started to crawl down the burrow.

'Rabbits must be mad to live down here!' he thought

'I wonder where the light switch is? I can't see a thing.'

When Melany-Jane came back there was a terrible noise coming from the burrow. She rushed over and peered down.

"Oliver are you all right?" she asked.

"No I am not!" was the cross reply.

"Well come back and we'll find somewhere else" she said.

"I can't."

"Why?"

"Because I'm stuck that's why!"

"Stay there and I'll try and pull you out"

"Stay there!?" repeated Oliver "What else can I do?

I'm S.T.U.C.K. Stuck!"

"Now, now, don't get hysterical" said Melany-Jane, trying hard to stay calm herself. She reached down into the tunnel and felt around for Oliver and eventually she found his tail. She heaved and pulled on it until she was red in the face but he was very firmly wedged and wouldn't move. "We might have to leave you there until you slim!" she shouted down to Oliver.

"Don't be silly!" came the cross reply "tortoises only get bigger they cant slim."

With that Melany-Jane grabbed hold of his tail and pulled even harder.

Oliver was just wondering if his tail would be as long as a mouse's, if he ever got out, when suddenly he shot backwards out of the hole, and flew through the air.

So did Melany-Jane much to her surprise.

"Well!" he said on landing "I don't think tortoises were meant to go down holes."

"No" agreed Melany-Jane, rubbing her back "I don't think they were."

"What are we going to do next?" asked Melany-Jane. They sat and thought again, at least Melany-Jane did Oliver went to sleep.

"I know!" she exclaimed picking Oliver up "I know you didn't like it on the ground so we'll see if you like it any better up in the air!" Oliver didn't think he liked the sound of that either but he was too tired to argue.

"Um, how am I going to hibernate in the air?" he asked trying to be casual.

"Up in a tree" said Melany-Jane triumphantly.

"Up a what?" screamed Oliver.

"Err, up a tree" repeated Melany-Jane not so sure now.

"Well squirrels do it so why can't tortoises" She finished defensively.

"I'll tell you why can't tortoises" said Oliver "because they haven't got wings!"

"Neither have squirrels, they climb up to their dray and that's what you're going to do. I'll help of course."

"Oh well I suppose I'd better get it over with" grumbled Oliver.

They found a suitable tree. Melany-Jane had put her shoes on which were easy for climbing in. Up in the branches they could see a hole in the trunk.

"Ideal!" exclaimed Melany-Jane, she tucked Oliver into her belt and began to climb up. This wasn't a good idea because he kept slipping out and he became quite nervous.

In the end they decided that Melany-Jane should climb up first and haul Oliver up after on a rope.

"I only hope none of me friends are watching this I'd never live it down!"

Melany-Jane was having a spot of bother in the branches.

She could pull on the rope or she could keep hold of the branches.

But she could not do both together.

First she let go of the branches.

Which gave her quite a shock.

Then she let go of the rope.

Which gave Oliver quite a shock.

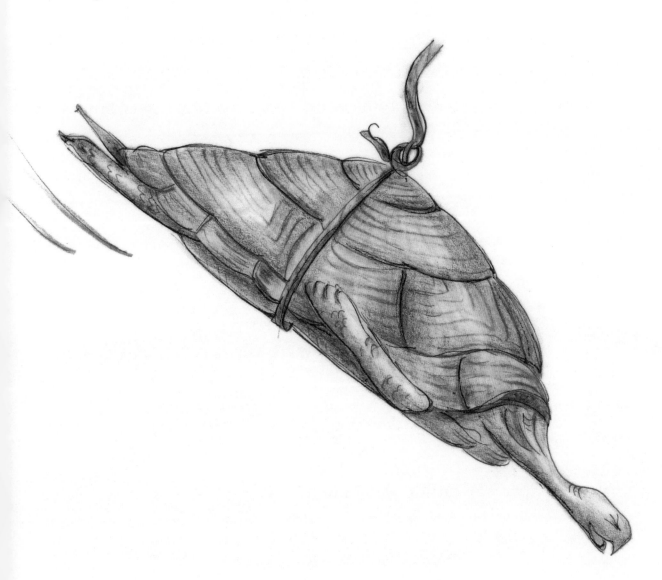

Then she let go of everything.

Which gave them both quite a shock and she fell screaming from the tree.

She had a soft but rather wet landing.

Oliver looked down at her and said "Do you know what, I don't think tortoises would like to hibernate in a pond either."

Melany-Jane was not at all pleased.

"OLIVER!" screamed Melany-Jane "I've got a good mind to stuff you into a box and forget about you."
Oliver thought about it. "That would be cosy' he said sighing.

Melany-Jane was amazed "Why didn't I think of it before?" she asked "we've got an old box that we could stuff with straw to keep you warm and we could puncture it with air-holes so that you can breath."
"Ah bliss!" said Oliver dreamily.

So that's what she did and then put it in a safe place in the garage. Then she took Oliver to inspect his new home, he was impressed.

"Just right!" he said "Just right!" and snuggled down deep into the straw.

"See you next spring" he said.

"Yes, see you next spring" said Melany-Jane a bit tearfully

"Oh! And Oliver..."

"Um?"

"Sweet dreams!"

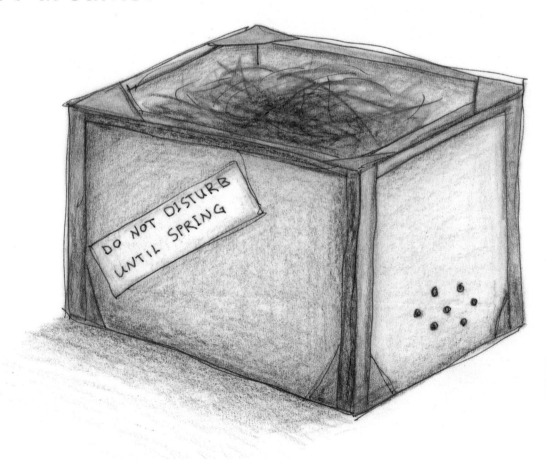

Printed in Great Britain
by Amazon

11368932R00016